Parallel Encounters
Allegiance

Book 3

David Scott Fields II

Thrive
Christian Press

Jupiter, Florida
www.thrivechristianpress.com

Thrive Christian Press
1095 Military Trail #8584
Jupiter, Florida 33468

First published by Thrive Christian Press on September 20, 2015.

ISBN 978-0-692-37545-7

Published and printed in the United States of America.

Dedication

This book is dedicated to Jason and Sarah Sheets, who are taking on the world for Christ. May He walk with you and your family each and every day!

Reader's Note

The following adventure takes place one year after the events chronicled in *Parallel Encounters: Salvage*, and approximately one month after the *Prism's Echo* was first discovered on Staranana. Let the reader be warned - the villain in this story is unlike any I have ever created before.

Before

"Oh, my goodness! Didn't that banana bread smell amazing?" Sparkey Moonbeam lauded.

"It sure did! And did you see that *turkey?* At least, it looked like a turkey. It was as big as me!" Scotty Fields exclaimed.

"Chef Berry told me it's called a *gramin*. It's a fat, flightless bird from the jungles of Stararocka. Captain Noble had two dozen of them sent here for the *Thanksgiving* feast. Chef has been slow cooking them since before we got lost in the past."

"That's been over a month! Well, from everyone here's perspective, anyway. I guess for us it has been about seven months."

"We're expecting nearly three hundred at the feast, and I doubt those things cook very quickly."

"True, but they have my mouth watering nonetheless, and *Thanksgiving* is still four days away. Are you sure your mom will be okay with me joining you guys for dinner? It's hard enough just to get a snack out of Chef these days."

"You're kidding right? My mom and dad love having you over, Scotty. Besides, my mom loves cooking. I think she misses doing it now that Chef Berry feeds us most days."

"Well, I'm certainly bringing an appetite. What are we having?"

"Iced trout boiled in plume berry juice."

Sparkey Moonbeam watched his best friend's face twist with disgust. Scotty was no fan of fish – and this was no secret. If anything, he and fish were the bitterest of enemies. Shortly after they had first met, Scotty had choked down a single iced trout for the sheer sake of survival. He and Sparkey had been in the aqueducts at the time, and the lighting had been fairly poor, but Sparkey had sworn his friend's face turned positively green!

"Ha! I'm just kidding. My mom knows you better than that. We're having *tacos*!"

"Tacos! Those are my favorite, but even Chef Berry hasn't made them for me, and I don't remember bringing any of the ingredients back with me from Earth."

"Let's just say, it involved some collusion with TB's historical database from when he was on Earth and an ultra-secret supply run to Stararocka. They have something like cheese there and an animal that I have been told tastes something like beef."

"This should be interesting!"

"Yeah, and we're already late. Let's get going!"

~

The soft white Starananian sun had already set by the time Sparkey and Scotty entered the spacious Moonbeam apartment within the Palace. The place was bigger than Scotty's home back on Earth, so he often forgot that his friends had spent most of their lives living in a small and damp cave deep within the frozen Nana Forest. Thus, despite its lavish size, the apartment was modestly furnished with a simple couch, a few sitting chairs, a hand carved table, and a wolf-skin rug. One thing that was rather spectacular though was the window!

Cosmic Bubble Palace was ancient in the extreme – over 1,000,000 Starananian years old. No one quite agreed who had built it. Most said it had been the first emperor, Iren, but since it had existed since before Iren and the bears assumed physical form, that seemed unlikely. The more likely theory was that it had been constructed by the hand of the Hidden King – God Himself. Were his life to endure another 1,000 years, Scotty doubted he would have enough time to unlock all the secrets concealed within its hoary walls. However, one thing that was not so secret was that virtually every room in the Palace had a spectacular view.

Almost every chamber from the 10th floor to the 100th was equipped with at least one twenty-foot-long bay window. Most of those windows looked out over hundreds of miles of snow littered forest. The highest were wrapped in a blanket of clouds that tinged orange, red, and purple with the setting sun. And those facing north were greeted each morning with the crashing tides of the Ice Sea.

When the rebellion and Scotty had overthrown Seth and his goons, all the rebels had moved into the Palace. The Moonbeams had chosen chambers with just such a view, and at this very moment, Gloria Moonbeam was staring out the window. Oddly though, with the sun having set, the sea would no longer be visible. Sparkey suspected, at first, that she was staring at the spectacular star scape out tonight, but no. Her gaze was directed toward the ground.

"Hey, Mama. What are you doing?' Sparkey Moonbeam asked as he and Scotty approached Gloria.

"Huh? Oh, hello, boys," Gloria said, and her countenance was notably fallen.

"What's the matter, Gloria?" Scotty asked, even as he and Sparkey took up positions beside her at the window. They both looked toward the ground, and 20 stories below in the northern courtyard, they could just make out three torches glowing in the hands of three bears.

"Who's down there?" Scotty asked.

"Spikey, General Shortstop, and Colonel Speedway."

"What are they doing?" Sparkey asked.

"Tonight, it's been 17 years."

"17 years?" Scotty inquired.

"17 years ago, tonight, 100 bears lost their lives because of the betrayal of Kelcott."

"Oh…I'm so sorry."

Gloria put her hand on the human boy's shoulder and rubbed his back gently. "You have nothing to be sorry about, Scotty. Through you, Christ has brought so much joy to this world in the last two years that finally, this year, this anniversary almost passed without being noticed."

"Almost?"

"The General's father died that night. I don't think he'll ever forget…nor should he. Since he, Speedway, and Spikey were the only witnesses to survive that night of horror, they decided to have a private vigil so as not to disrupt the festive atmosphere."

Scotty's head hung, and he almost wished he hadn't decided to bring *Thanksgiving* to Staranana. It would have been more appropriate to spend this time in somber remembrance than in celebratory feasting. Still, Gloria did not allow the melancholy of the moment to last.

"Anyway, sorry, boys. You're not here for sad old memories. You're here for tacos!"

"Boy, yeah!" Scotty beamed, and his grin was ear to ear.

"I hope you like them. They're my own special recipe. Call them *Tacos a la Moonbeam.*"

"Gloria, you could make even fish taste good," Scotty smirked and gave a wink to Sparkey.

They all headed into the Moonbeams' modest kitchen area and slid into chairs around the table. The taco fixings were already in place, and Scotty could barely restrain himself from instantly digging in. Some of the ingredients he recognized, but others were entirely new. There was a shredded, waxy substance that Scotty guessed was a version of cheese, though it was red. The *beef* was actually a stringier meat than he had ever seen before – though pulled pork bore a close resemblance. One dish of diced blue vegetables stung his eyes as he caught a whiff of them, and he guessed they were the Stararockan equivalent of onions. The tomatoes – or what he took to be tomatoes – were green, and there were more than a dozen other toppings he could not entirely place at the moment.

"Gloria, this is way above and beyond for a simple sleepover!" Scotty beamed.

"Well, taste a few before you offer too much praise."

"Will Spikey be joining us?"

"Not for a while. He told me not to wait on him. Now, let's eat!"

The table was soon rattling with the passing of plates and the clinking of glasses. Taco enthusiast that he was, Scotty did his best to fill his tortilla [an orange flatbread] with almost every topping on the table. Only when the first taco fell apart halfway to his mouth did he hesitate and say, "Um, maybe we should pray first."

Gloria smiled and said, "Good idea! Do you mind doing the honors?"

"Not at all," Scotty said. Then he prayed, "Lord, we love you so much, and we thank you for this food. We also thank you for the memories of old friends. Though we won't see them for a while, we eagerly await the day when we will, so please, Lord Jesus, come quickly. Amen!"

"Amen!" Sparkey and Gloria echoed.

They began digging into their meal, and by the time Scotty was halfway through his sixth *alien* taco, Gloria had few doubts left about her recipe being a success. In fact, had Scotty's mouth been empty long enough to say it, he would have told her that his dad [the Fields family's taco-making genius] would have been proud of her. That is, if he had actually known she existed.

His belly finally full, Scotty sat back in his chair and sighed. Then he said, "That was amazing, Gloria! Spikey doesn't know what he missed, and…" The boy paused as his eyes fell on a strange and tattered book resting on the countertop near the table.

"Is that what I think it is?" the emperor asked.

"Uh…um…" Gloria stuttered.

"Out with it, Gloria!"

Gloria's shoulders slumped, and she surrendered, "Yes, it's the *Prism's Echo*. Spikey and Nicodemus have been testing its abilities."

"I know that, but what is it doing all askew in your kitchen?"

"Spikey told me they have asked it about twenty different questions now, and they are getting closer each time to not losing themselves in the narrative. One of them always stands by while the other asks the question, and they don't let each other stay in the story longer than a minute. Eventually, Spikey wanted to test the book on something a little different than a fictional narrative. He asked me to pose a medical scenario to it."

"What happened?"

"I asked it about a young she-bear who died in childbirth about seven years ago. I was only a medical assistant at the time. The doctor in charge of the delivery diagnosed her with a glucose imbalance. That's why she was losing the strength and will to deliver. I said I suspected an internal hemorrhage. The doctor wouldn't listen, and she died."

"That's horrible! Were you right?"

"We obviously didn't have the correct equipment to diagnose something like that back then, but there are certain roots in the forest that have a potent ability to stem a hemorrhage – internal or otherwise. The *Prism's Echo* let me try them, and the girl lived."

"I wish it could have been real life. Whatever happened to that doctor?"

"He was killed in a goon raid about three years later. That's when I became head doctor of the rebellion."

Scotty stood and approached the *Prism's Echo*. He placed a single hand on its rough leather cover.

"Scotty, what are you thinking?" Sparkey asked.

"About my friends in the other universe."

"Here we go again," Gloria quipped. "What is it this time?"

"Well, people in this life make lots of mistakes, and sometimes people even betray each other – like Kelcott did. As a result, people often die."

"This is sure turning into a real cheery evening!" Sparkey sneered.

"I'm know; I'm sorry. I'm just wondering how my friends would deal with a traitor in their midst?"

Chapter 1
Jess A. Bell

Although the bridge was already impenetrably dark, their captain's face was even darker. Her golden skin was stiff, and her slanted eyes burned with rage. Before her, on the static filled viewer, was the image of a single *SYCO* class vessel being slaughtered by a small rebel cruiser. Through the static, she took in the visage of the attacking vessel. Small, with abrupt lines along its fuselage and a slanted forward section, it seemed hardly a threat to the massive *SYCO* ship, but within the densely packed lunar system of Jupiter's orbit, the tiny craft was doing far more than its share of damage to the Nazi vessel.

Suddenly, the screen went black, and a stream of profanities bled from her lips before she asked, "What just happened?"

A young Nazi, barely in his mid-teens, with ebony hair and a smooth complexion spoke her name, "Captain Bell, the holoviewer's circuits have burned out. It will take several hours to repair them. We never should have tried to push their range so far."

She stood and moved closer to him. Her slender and curving body caused every hormone within the young lieutenant to throb with desire, but he knew she was no prize to be sought. Her full name was Jessica Alice Bell, but everyone called her Jess A. Bell – a name which bore a striking resemblance to the biblical villainess named Jezebel. And like her biblical counterpart, Captain Bell was every bit the demon.

Known throughout the solar system for her intense *appetites*, she was both feared and sought by men and women alike for an evening of surreal pleasure that more often than not ended in death – and everyone who entered her chambers knew that and didn't care.

Bell had no moral center, and she would not hesitate to kill anyone. Her former commander on the *RSS Breakaway* had learned that the hard way. Yes, at one point, she had been a rebel, a refugee from Mars. But on the very mission where the *RSS Breakaway* had been rechristened the *Intruder* something had changed. The mission had ended with the *Breakaway's* captain dead and Bell a traitor. Her motives remained a mystery to all even to this day eight years later. But there was no question that since that time she had indulged in every kind of depravity a human being was capable of enjoying.

The pulse of the young lieutenant, Daniel Brandon, throbbed harder as Bell placed a single hand on his shoulder and rubbed it gently. Her scent alone was almost worth dying for. It seemed to call out to him just as the song of the Sirens had once called out to Odysseus, but no small part of him was still terrified. However, when a grin broadened across her face, he allowed himself to relax ever so slightly.

She inquired softly, "You said several hours, Lieutenant?"

"Yes, Captain."

Her smile didn't even fade as she slapped the back of her hand across his face, and he crashed to the floor. "Then get it done!"

Brandon did not immediately rise back to his feet. Instead, he waddled over to his control board on his knees and removed a panel from beneath it. Once the circuitry was exposed, he set to work. However, his thoughts were not on the task he suspected his very life now depended on, but rather on how his life could have possibly brought him to this point.

His parents and their parents before them had been members of the New Nazi cult – all of whom were waiting for the return of the god-like Saki Chu. For all his life, he had been instructed in the propaganda of the cult, but his heart had never been in it. The first time he had ever killed someone, he had had nightmares for months afterward. And he did not support the Nazi philosophy of producing a master race. He had made this decision when his best friend at the age of eight was dragged from his home by Nazi cult members and beaten until dead – just because he was Jewish.

Brandon had thought such horrific prejudices long dead, and even the New Nazi Confederation typically distanced itself from hate crimes of the like. Unlike Adolf Hitler, Saki Chu preferred the *inferiors* to die on the battlefield, so this new regime lacked the concentration camps of the days of old. Even so, before even his first whisker had sprouted, Daniel Brandon had decided that the Nazis were an evil worth nothing less than total destruction.

Had he been born off world, he would have joined the rebellion in an instant. As it was, he was born in what remained of New York City to very loyal Nazi parents. Eventually, years of conditioning and their lies left him with little choice but to submit to the life fate had dealt him. When the war began, he had even enlisted and become a good little Nazi solider. Even so, somewhere, deep within him, the dream of freedom and truth still burned – waiting for a chance to break free.

Jess A. Bell settled back into her command chair and tossed her flowing black hair over her shoulder. She asked, "What is the name of the attacking vessel?"

A rugged Nazi officer, with the tiniest hints of a beard on his face answered her, "It's the *RSS Intruder*."

"The *SYCO* butcher! I should have known. It's been a long time."

The bearded Nazi, a Commander Samuel Pfeiffer, asked, "Do you still know anyone onboard?"

"I doubt Lori Brooks would ever forget me," Bell said, and she let out a string of expletives describing the *Intruder's* captain that Brandon cringed to hear, but after that she fell silent. Everyone knew she had once been a rebel, and it had been her supposed murder of the rebel Captain Brian Morgan that had earned her a place among the Nazis. Even so, any further details about her separation from the rebels she kept quiet, even now, eight years removed from the incident. Whatever had happened that day, it had awoken a demon within Jess A. Bell – a demon with only one purpose – revenge!

Pfeiffer reported, "Captain, our vessel may be small enough to traverse the lunar field and let us intercept the *Intruder*."

A wicked grin curled Bell's lip. Destroying the *Intruder* would be immensely gratifying. For whatever reason, the gods seemed to look with favor on that vessel and its crew. They had now held the Nazi Space Port for nearly five years, and the vessel they had just obliterated marked the third *SYCO* class vessel on their kill list. Only the *Berserko* had managed to escape (rumor had it with some incredible alien technology), but they had instantly gone into hiding.

Needless to say, the presence of the Nazis beyond Earth was dwindling rapidly, but if she could retake the Space Port that would all change. The *Intruder* was the key to that onslaught and to final and complete victory.

She turned to the rugged commander and said, "Thank you, Sam." Then she met his eyes with a smile that promised far more than words ever could in that moment.

Her ship, the *Feline's Claw*, was smaller than most Nazi spacecraft, but it was also far more powerful. Consisting of seven decks and a fifty-six-person crew, the ship had weapons comparable to those of three *SYCO* class vessels combined. Eight laser cannons, four thousand thermonuclear missiles, and one hundred tachyon pulse projectiles comprised her armaments. All were perfectly aligned along her hull, which was the shape of an old-fashioned orbital capsule – curved along the back and extending forward in a cone shape. Along with a complicated array of thrusters, allowing nanosecond responses in maneuvering, and a computer system based on neural fiber processing technology, she was a vessel to be reckoned with. Bell felt confident that the destruction of the *Intruder* would be a quick and efficient task.

Chapter 2
Taken

Emperor Scotty Fields felt dizzy, but he stilled himself against *The Prism's Echo's* blinding aura. Once again, he had been unprepared for its sudden reaction to his question. The book hadn't even been open this time, but that didn't seem to matter. It had sucked him in, and he hoped he would find himself back among his friends again; but something felt very different this time. He was not *himself*. The awkward, pre-teen body he knew had been transformed. He was taller, his shoulders were broader, and his muscles were thicker – much thicker. His reality was also blowing away like sand in the wind, but he just kept repeating to himself, "I will remember...I will remember who I am!"

And then he heard the applause.

He was standing on the bridge of what he remembered to be the *Intruder*, and the entire bridge crew was standing and applauding and cheering for him. He had no clue why for only an instant, and then, as if he had been hit by the full force of a river that had just broken through a dam, Emperor Scotty Fields was washed out of existence, and only Lt. Scott Fields remained.

Lt. Fields took a less than modest bow. Once again, the *Ram-charge Maneuver* had saved the day, but this time, the maneuver was not the only credit to their victory. One year earlier, Agent Loso and Chief Martinez had stolen the plans for more than a dozen new alien technologies from an alien vessel called the *Rimcha*. Since that time, the Space Port's defenses had been brought up to full strength, and the *Intruder's* systems had received several major upgrades; not the least of which was a new array of alien armaments. Now the ship was more than a match for any *SYCO* class vessel.

Even Loso, who had literally done nothing during the battle, took a little bit of the credit when he said, "The alien pulse cannons I scanned and adapted for our ship did do a significant amount of damage. Please don't take all the credit, Lt. Fields."

Brooks stood and, with a smile and two raised hands, silenced her crew. She said, "Congratulations, everyone. The Nazi vessel *Weirdo* didn't get anywhere near our base on Io, thanks to the efforts of this crew, but let's not forget the real reason we returned to Jupiter."

With those words, she turned to the young Latin who stood in the far rear corner of the bridge. Directing him to come toward her, she said, "Before we left the base this morning, I received the official clearance and authorization I know we all feel is long overdue. Last month, at the behest of Admiral Carter and myself, this young man did what no other rebel has done since we captured the Space Port. He stole Nazi technology directly from a Confederation vessel. And this was no ordinary technology; it was the Nazi's highly classified portal teleportation device – a piece of equipment that will allow us to plant troops on Nazi controlled bases from great distances and greatly reduce the risks to our own ships. I don't need to remind any of you of how long the rebellion has been trying to get its hands on such technology. Well, this young man achieved that goal, and not only that, but he also lived to talk about it."

She spoke his name, "Chief Klaus Martinez, for outstanding services to the rebellion, it is my pleasure to wave your enlisted status and grant you a full commission as a lieutenant commander in the Anti-Nazi Rebellion Forces." Then, extending her arm, she placed a brass tag on the collar of his uniform. In well-polished letters, the tag displayed his new rank.

As his modesty was overwhelmed by his continually reddening face, Brooks took hold of his hand and said, "Congratulations, Lt. Commander," and then the entire bridge erupted with cheers and applause once more.

Lt. Fields was the first at Martinez's side and he said, "Well, I guess I'll have to call you *sir* from now on. Just don't let it go to your head!" Then he smiled and said, "Great job, Klaus."

Martinez returned the smile, and Fields headed back to the helm. He had a report to finish, and he had never been one for procrastinating; but what he found at the helm was not a collection of unfinished forms. Rather, it was a flashing alarm beacon!

"Captain!"

Brooks turned from Klaus and asked, "What is it?"

"There's *another* Nazi vessel on an attack approach!"

"Battle stations, everyone!" Brooks commanded.

Her crew moved seamlessly to their stations, and she noted not a tinge of panic on a single face. Nazi attacks were becoming rather routine, but it now seemed years since the *Intruder* and her crew had gotten the short end of the deal.

Commander Leah Smith reported, "This is not a *SYCO* class vessel, Captain. It's a stealth suicide capsule. I've only seen a few of them in my day. They look very much like warheads, and their original purpose was suicide runs. Essentially, the ship is one giant bomb. The defenses of the Mars Colony were annihilated with the impact of three of these ships. The blast radius from each vessel extended over 500 kilometers. After that, it was only a matter of hours before the rest of the colony fell."

"And these things have human crews?" Brooks questioned.

Loso answered, "Most were manned by B.O.Ts., Captain. Though I do remember reading reports about some of the more *insane* humans among the Nazi ranks being assigned aboard a few."

"It is also likely that after our blockade of Earth, the Nazis left in the solar system have exchanged crew members from time to time. Let's hope that makes this ship less likely to indulge in a suicide run," Smith hoped.

"What's its name?" Brooks asked.

"Its registry identifies it as the *Nazi Confederation Vessel (NCV) Feline's Claw.*"

Brooks had never heard of the vessel, but she was not about to let that worry her. She instructed her crew, "All right, we've done this before. Just stay focused on your jobs, and we'll get through this like all the rest."

Her first officer, Commander Caleb Eli reported, "The captain of that vessel is hailing us."

"Put the signal on the holoviewer, Commander."

As Eli did so, the holographic clone of a slender Asian woman materialized before them. With a hint of the devil in her demeanor, she said, "My name is Captain…"

"Jess A. Bell," Brooks interrupted her. "I remember you. Though you were an ensign the last time we met."

Bell smirked, "Lower your defenses, Captain, and prepare to surrender your ship."

"Or…"

"Or we will destroy you!"

Even as Brooks allowed Bell's threat to sink in, she noticed the reactions of her crew. Despite the fact that the woman before them was only a hologram, she could hear the accelerated breathing of every male member of her bridge crew. The creature before them was possibly one of the most attractive women they had ever seen.

Brooks only rolled her eyes and then said, "Perhaps you haven't been keeping up with the latest news, Captain. The rebels have bottled the Nazis up on Earth, and we're making swift work of the few of your vessels that remain in the solar system these days."

Then, making a slashing gesture across her throat, she signaled Eli to cut off the channel. She ordered, "Commander Smith, target their vessel's engines with tachyon pulses. Let them know we mean business."

Smith did so, and a full round of five tachyon pulses ripped into the *Feline's Claw*. "Direct hit, Captain! We should launch…"

Before her tactical officer could finish that sentence, Brooks found herself being launched across the bridge as the bulkhead beneath her feet exploded. Instantly, another half-dozen consoles erupted in white hot flames.

"Captain, are you all right?" Smith yelled over the roar around her.

"I'll live. How is every…oh, no! Smith…Eli!" Brooks exclaimed and pointed to the limp form of her first officer on the deck. He was blood smeared and unmoving. Even as another round of enemy fire pelted the *Intruder*, Smith knelt down and felt the Commander's neck. There was a slight pulse. Relieved, she reported, "The Commander is alive, Captain, but I don't think any of us will be for much longer. The *Feline's Claw* has scored several direct hits. We have massive hull breaches, and the causality reports keep coming. The good news is I still have weapons control, Captain. Should I return fire?"

"Fire at will, Commander!"

Then she stumbled down to the helm. Struggling past twisted metal debris, she reached Lt. Fields and shouted over the deafening cacophony of the battle, "This vessel is more of a threat than I thought. Do you think we can use the *Ram-charge*?"

For Fields, the *Ram-charge* was becoming something of a routine, but they would have no such luck in using it this time. He shouted back, "No, Captain. The Nazis have destroyed our thruster array. We still have the Light Speed Drive, but that is too fast for the maneuver. It could get us of out of here though, Captain!"

Brooks locked her eyes on the holoviewer which now displayed the attacking vessel. Though the ship was smaller than the *Intruder*, it was proving more than a match. Struggling back toward Smith, she hoped the commander was having some success. She inquired, "Attack status?"

Smith continued to adjust her controls with heat blistered hands and said, "Dismal, Captain. That vessel is too heavily shielded."

Brooks turned back to the holoviewer and watched the *Feline's Claw* continue to assault the *Intruder*, even as Loso reported, "Fourteen crew members are dead. Ten of those were sucked into space through the breaches. We are leaking tachyons into space, and all systems are losing power. If we are going to retreat, we must do it now."

Brooks had never been the running away type, but as the Nazi ship continued to pound its weapons against her vessel, it seemed hopeless. She ordered Fields, "Take us out of here at full LS, Lieutenant."

"Aye, Cap…"

Her command had come just one instant too late, and she watched as her teenage helmsman went soaring from his station and landed at her feet in a charred and bloody heap. Brooks had little doubt he was dead, but she hesitated to confirm it. Instead, she only waited as Smith reported, "Five Nazi TSJs have just entered the ship through the breaches and more soldiers are appearing out of nowhere on every deck!"

"Portal technology?" Brooks questioned.

"It must be, Captain."

"Let's get the wounded to the escape pods. We have to get out of here. Signal the crew to abandon ship. If we can maneuver the pods into the lunar debris field, we should be able to hide until help arrives."

"Aye, Captain!" Smith complied as she activated the evacuation claxon.

Loso gathered Commander Eli in his arms. Brooks could see shrapnel protruding from the skulls and chests of four crew members between her and the helm. There was no question they were dead, but she still could not bring herself to confirm Lt. Fields' demise.

"Captain, we have to get out of here!" Martinez shouted at her.

"You all go. I have to check on, Lieutenant…"

Her voiced was drowned out as a high-pitched chime suddenly filled the air of the bridge. Then there was a ripple of blue light and ten Nazis, including Bell herself, appeared out of thin air.

Brooks allowed a wicked and defiant smile to shape on her lips, and then with as much sarcasm as she could muster, she sneered, "Welcome back to the *Intruder*, Jess A. Bell!"

Bell, armed with a hellish Nazi rifle, gave Brooks one of her own deadly smiles and then slammed her across the face with the butt of the rifle. Brooks fell to the floor and her head came to an abrupt stop on the deck in a pool of blood puddled next to Lt. Fields.

"Your vessel is mine now, Captain. You and your crew will be executed."

Then she placed a single slender finger along the side of her mouth and looking very coy said, "You know, at first, I just wanted to destroy your ship. Eliminating the butcher of the *SYCO* would no doubt earn me a thing or two from the Confederation. But then I thought of how much fun it might be to torture the lot of you. At the very least, I owe *you* that much, Captain."

"That was a long time ago! I had no other choice, but to report your…"

"Save your lies. I've heard enough of them to last a lifetime."

"Only the truly deranged see the truth as a lie."

Bell ignored this and instead said, "I intend to torture and kill every member of your crew, Captain. And you're going to watch while I do it. Right up until I kill you."

Bell then looked down at the charred flesh of Lt. Fields, and Brooks was surprised to hear, "I'll start with him."

At that, a Nazi officer, with an unusual softness in his eyes, helped Lt. Fields to his feet. *He was still alive!* Grievously wounded, but alive!

Brooks demanded, "Stop! If anyone is to suffer, it will be me. Leave my crew out of it!"

"Unlikely, Captain, but if it will make you feel any better, I'll make sure you suffer more than they do. Now, get him out of here, Lieutenant."

As Bell watched her officer lead Fields away, Brooks pushed herself back to her knees. Ordinarily, in this circumstance, she would have kept her eyes locked on the doomed teen until the last possible second. A sign of respect? Perhaps. An unspoken call for him to stay strong? Certainly. But in this instance, something else had caught her attention, and she didn't think Fields would mind in the least. Directly below her knees was a small panel marked in three bold red words – *Helm Relay Junction.*

"Thank you, Lord!" she prayed silently as realization struck. Though the rebels tended to make their helms virtually indestructible, they recognized that nothing was perfect, and in a war like this, losing helm control was unacceptable. Thus, they had equipped each rebel vessel with dozens of auxiliary helm relays, located throughout the ship. One had to have command clearance to access them, which Brooks obviously did. She would have only seconds before Bell's attention would be back on her.

Throwing open the panel, she moved her slender hands like lightning through a series of tangled wires and wrapped her hands around a tiny lever. Then she remembered Fields's report that only the LS Drive was still online. If that was true, the next few seconds were going to get a little bumpy, but she was not about to let Bell make good on her plans. She tapped what appeared to be several random controls on the side of the panel and pulled the lever.

What happened next was all a blur.

In an almost dream like haze, Brooks saw Bell crash to the deck beside her as the *Intruder* shot instantly to light speed. The sudden surge of velocity had overwhelmed the ship's gravity generators momentarily and sent everyone tumbling to the deck – *Brooks hoped with no injuries*. On the holoviewer, the planet Jupiter swelled beyond its normal gigantic size, until the enflamed gases of her fiery atmosphere had consumed the *Intruder*. For a single fraction a second longer, the rebel ship continued to plunge through a mesh of hydrogen and methane. All the while, the pressure outside the ship was building, threatening to crush the imperiled vessel.

When the ship finally halted, Bell was the first on her feet. "What did you just do?" she raged and spat a series of expletives.

After tapping a few more controls, Brooks stood, and met Bell's cold eyes. "I have taken us into Jupiter's atmosphere. We are now thousands of kilometers from orbital altitudes. I have also locked out the helm with an encryption code. You will not be able to take this vessel back into space, and if you don't surrender it within one day, we will have fallen so deep into the atmosphere that you'll see Hell before you see home again."

"Fine, have it your way!" raged Bell. Pointing to Smith, she ordered her men, "Kill her now!"

But before the Nazi could carry out her orders, Brooks shook her head and said, "I wouldn't do that if I were you."

"Oh, no?" Bell sneered.

Brooks smirked, "Nope, definitely not a good idea. You see, I had the computer select a single person on this crew and I had it lock out the helm with their personal security code. Even I don't know who that person is, and only they can unlock the helm. So, if you kill even one of them, you run the risk of losing the code. But I can assure you, none of them will surrender their codes without my direct order, and that's one order I don't intend to give. If you want to live, I suggest you leave my ship now!"

Bell smiled and countered, "I have my own ways of extracting information. Ways that can be both painful and pleasant. And besides, the *Feline's Claw* can have us out of here in less than an hour. You've failed, Captain."

"Oh, is that a fact. I don't suppose, the *Feline's Paw...*" Brooks started.

"*Claw!*" Bell barked.

"Oh, excuse me. I don't suppose your ship is equipped with a Black Vortex Matrix?"

"What are you getting at?" Bell asked.

"It's just that, conventional thrusters won't be enough for them to come even within portaling range. And if they try to use the matrix, chances are they'll be sucked straight to the planet's core."

Bell squirmed. Brooks was right; there was no way the *Feline's Claw* would be able to approach them. She would have to depend on the resources presently at hand to get this vessel back to the Confederation. Then she suddenly had an incredibly enticing idea. She turned to one of her officers, "Ensign, you and your men take the *Intruder's* crew to the mess hall. Keep them under guard, but do not harm them unless they give you a reason to. Then find Lt. Brandon and tell him he has a change of orders. Tell him to take that young lieutenant to his quarters and have him post a guard. Then he is to report to the mess hall and guard the prisoners with the rest of the men. I will be stopping by later on to personally speak to the young man."

The ensign nodded and carried out his orders. As he led Brooks away, the captain gazed at Bell, wondering what she could be planning. Though she had every confidence in Scott, he was only human. So, whether Bell planned to use some form of seduction or inhuman torture, she hoped the young man could resist. For all their sakes, she hoped he could.

Chapter 3
Church

Commander Eli awoke to the touch of a cool cotton cloth upon his forehead. Pressing his temple hard, he tried to focus in on his surroundings, but to no avail. Objects spun in a chaotic haze about his head so quickly that his stomach churned and poured its contents upward.

"Easy, Commander," came a gentle voice. "You took a nasty blow."

Eli pressed his temple again, and after a moment, the haze clarified to become the beautiful visage of Commander Leah Smith. When he could finally look at her and not feel the overwhelming urge to vomit (not the best compliment to his crush), he asked, "What happened?"

"The Nazi ship turned out to be more of a threat than expected. The *Intruder* suffered heavy damage in the attack, and we lost a lot of people."

Eli tried to sit up, but it only aggravated his head wound, so Smith helped him. When he saw the swirling gases through the mess hall viewport he had to ask, "From the look of that, I take it we're…?"

"Inside Jupiter's atmosphere. During the attack, some of the Nazi crew came over and took control of the ship.

The helm was destroyed, so Captain Brooks used a relay to pilot us here. Then she locked out the controls with an encryption code. The computer will only disengage the helm lockout if a certain security code is entered - a code which matches the security code of some unknown person on our crew. Without the code, the Nazis can't pilot the ship out of here."

"Why are we in the mess hall?"

"Captain Brooks programmed the computer to lock out the helm the way she did so that the Nazis could not risk killing any of us. If they did, they'd run the risk of losing the code. When the Nazi captain realized our captain had outwitted her, she had her men bring us here while she decides what to do with us," Leah whispered softly as a Nazi officer walked by them, tachyon rifle in tow.

Eli's thoughts swam chaotically through his mind. All this seemed too much for him to take in while in his present condition. Rather than trying to make sense of what was going on, he decided to settle for a new topic of conversation. With a smile, he asked, "So, does this qualify as our first date?"

"Sure," she said. "And I can definitely say I have never had a more charming caller. I've got the vomit on my boots to prove it."

Eli smiled at that, even as he cringed as another surge of pain blasted through his head.

~

On the other side of the room, Captain Brooks stood with Chief Engineer Josh Austin, Loso, and Lt. Commander Martinez. She asked, "What were the exact losses in the battle?"

Loso reported, "Chief Austin lost his entire engineering crew. The hull breaches were massive, and it is unlikely our propulsion system will be able to get us out of here in its present state."

"Leave that to the Nazis. I overheard a status report. The ship is well on the way to being repaired," Brooks said.

Austin, who was still shaken by the loss of his staff, asked, "Captain, are you sure the Nazis won't be able to override the helm lockout?"

"Not a chance. Even if they knew the code, the helm would only respond to the person to whom the code belongs. Our problem will be retaking the ship before we sink too low in the atmosphere."

Martinez, whose gaze had been fixed on a Nazi whose name they had learned was Lt. Brandon, finally spoke, "What about him?"

Brooks turned to look at the Nazi. Though his expression surrendered no emotions, she read discontent in his eyes. "I think he might prove useful."

"Captain, are you suggesting that we play on his perceived malcontent and use him to help us retake the ship?" Loso whispered in his clipped mechanical voice.

Brooks was not accustomed to using people in the way Loso had just described. Even if this young man was a Nazi, she was still a Christian, and she had a standard to uphold. She replied, "No, but if we can find some way to reach him, maybe he would be willing to help us if we help him. We could offer him freedom from the Confederation and a new life with us."

"That's assuming we're right about him. He could be just as bloodthirsty as the rest of them," Austin pointed out.

"I suspect, if we scratched deep enough, we'd find discontent in most of the Nazis. When you're fed a steady diet of lies, murder, and cruelty, I imagine it would be hard not to feel your soul being chipped away a little bit at a time," Brooks said, her eyes still on Brandon.

"I don't think that Captain Bell has much of a soul left to worry about," quipped Martinez.

"You might be surprised," Brooks whispered.

"What's her story, Captain?" Loso asked.

Brooks hesitated and then said, "It's a long one, and now perhaps isn't the best time. The short version is that I knew her a long time ago. She was a junior officer on the *Breakaway* – now the *Intruder*. Our captain at the time became enamored with her; the problem was he was already married. They had an affair, and I had the unfortunate privilege of walking in on them kissing in one of the maintenance closets. Regulations generally forbid a captain from becoming involved with a subordinate, and adultery is a court martial offense in the rebellion."

"But I thought Captain Morgan was killed on the mission that earned the *Breakaway* its new name. How could that have happened if he was stripped of command before that?" Austin questioned.

"He was killed on that mission. He…Oh, never mind the gossip for now. We have more important things to worry about, like how to get through to Brandon."

"Captain, if I may, I have idea," Martinez offered.

"Well, don't keep it to yourself, Commander."

"It's six o'clock, ma'am."

"Six…oh! Excellent idea, Klaus!"

"Care to fill us in, Captain?" Loso asked.

"Commander Eli's condition has stabilized, Captain. Dr. Radcliff is tending to him now, but we have many more wounded that require more advanced medical attention," Commander Smith reported as she approached their group.

Brooks said, "We'll just have to convince the Nazis to grant us access to sickbay, but I don't think that is going to happen at the moment." Then she turned to Austin and Martinez, ready to reveal her plan. With a smile, she instructed, "Gather all the Christian members of the crew together. Tell them we're going to have a good old fashioned worship service - just like the ones I remember from my childhood in Georgia."

Both Austin and Martinez were ecstatic about the idea and rushed off. Then Brooks turned to Smith and said, "Commander, I hope our worship service won't bother you."

Smith replied with a smile, "Captain, have you ever heard the expression *There are no atheists in a foxhole*? I think even I could use a little bit of God right about now, and this crew could use a whole lot of hope."

A grin the size of the Grand Canyon exploded across Brooks' face. She instructed, "Help Josh and Klaus get the crew together. I have a personal invitation I would like to deliver."

Smith was confused but didn't have time to comment as her captain suddenly headed toward the young Nazi that Captain Bell had called Lt. Brandon.

~

Lori Brooks was blunt, "My crew and I will be having a worship service while we wait."

Brandon started only slightly at the rebel captain's voice. He had been lost in thought, and he had honestly not noticed her approach. Had Bell been present, that little slipup may very well have cost him his life. Fortunately, none of the rest of the guards to seemed to notice. He adopted the smug demeanor the Nazis were legendary for and relaxed his rifle across his chest. With a shrug, he said, "I imagine that's a good idea. You'll all be dead soon anyway. Might as well make your peace with whatever force you believe in."

"For the record, we believe in Jesus the Christ, our Savior and Son of the Living God!"

"Whatever."

"Would you care to join us, Daniel?"

"How do you know my name?"

"I heard one of the other guards use it. Well?"

"Well, what?"

"Would you like to join us in worship?"

"Are you kidding? I'd be shot. Not to mention the fact that it's fairly ridiculous anyway. If it makes you feel better before we kill you, fine, but don't expect any of us to get involved."

"Oh, I wasn't asking the rest of them...just you, Lieutenant."

"Why?"

Brooks smiled, and as she turned to leave without answering his question, she said, "The invitation is always open." Then she headed back to the far side of the mess hall.

~

Never had a congregation come together with more efficiency. Within only moments of revealing Martinez's idea, Brooks' entire crew – believers and non-believers alike - was before her. Eager for a sense of hope, they all had their eyes fixed on her. Though she tended to spend these hours worshipping in solitude, she kept hearing over and over again in her spirit, *"For where two or three are gathered together in My name, I am there in the midst of them."*

She prayed silently, *"All right, Lord. Let's do this."* Then she began, "A few hours ago, I would never have conceived of us being in this situation, but here we are and I know our situation seems hopeless. But there will always be hope."

When her officers heard that, their eyes seemed to burn into her. They wanted very much to hear what this hope was. Even Smith, the atheist, seemed eager to hear more. Brooks continued, "Most of you already know this, even if you have yet to accept it, but that doesn't change its power and its truthfulness. This hope comes from Heaven – one place the Nazis never have and never will touch. Jesus Christ, God's own Son, gave it to us well over two thousand years ago, and it will be the power that allows us to retake our ship."

When Brandon heard that, his heart began to race. If he allowed a plan to retake the ship to unfold right before him and did nothing about it, Bell would certainly kill him, but for some reason he made no move to stop Brooks. In fact, when another Nazi moved to do so, Brandon ordered, "Take it easy, Ensign. Nothing is going to happen." Then he turned his attention back to the rebels and watched as Brooks went on.

Brooks said, "Our undeniable sense of security and hope comes from a passage in the *Bible, Luke 10:19*. Jesus made it clear to us when He said:

> *'Behold! I give you the authority to trample on serpents and scorpions, and over all the power of the enemy, and nothing shall by any means hurt you.'*

"This was a promise given to Christ's disciples as they ministered in His day, and while He was with them, and even long after that, they continued in that power and authority. Now, you may be asking what this has to do with us. Everything! For the same God that empowered those men stands with us now, and I declare in His Son's name that the crew of the *RSS Intruder* is claiming the promise of this passage. We will overcome the power of our enemies, and we will come through this alive and whole!" Then she turned and looked directly at Lt. Brandon and declared, "Not even the Nazis will be able to stop us!"

Brandon cringed, but he could not move or even speak in that moment. Brooks commanded, "Everyone on your feet!"

"Soldiers to arms!" shouted one of the Nazi ensigns, and with several sharp clicks more than a dozen tachyon rifles were directed at Brooks and her crew.

"We're just going to sing!" Brooks balked and defiantly turned her attention away from the guards poised to kill her crew.

Smith looked a little uncomfortable, though Brooks guessed it was more from the prospect of having to sing than from the guns pointing at her head. Even so, her tactical officer was the first to ask, "What are we going to sing, Captain?"

Brooks thought for a moment and then said, "I have always been partial to *Amazing Grace*, but it needs to be a little more upbeat than that."

Martinez put in, "Leave that to me, Captain. You start it off, and we'll all jump in."

Brooks began to sing, *"Amazing Grace, how sweet the sound that saved a wretch like me. I once was lost, but now I am found. Was blind but now I see…"*

And suddenly Klaus Martinez jumped in - hands clapping and feet stomping. A similar reaction cascaded through the entire crew, and soon they were all singing along. Making the somber old song more upbeat than it ever had been.

They sang out, *"I once was lost, but now I'm found - 'cause Jesus brought me home. I once was blind but now I see! My Lord Jesus has set me free. Just give me that Amazing Grace! What a sweet, sweet sound! Oh, that saved a wretch, yes a wretch like me! Oh, my Jesus, my sweet, sweet Jesus! My Savior set me free!"*

One officer rang out, "Sing it, sister!"

Then another called, "Amen, Captain!"

It was exactly like the worship services Brooks remembered from her childhood. Though her crew members came from a dozen different cultural backgrounds, that entire service cried out *Black Country Church*. And the longer they sang, the more smiles she saw break out among her people. Whatever tomorrow would bring seemed pointless. They were firmly in the hands of Christ. Captain Brooks only wished Lt. Fields could be here too.

Chapter 4
The Serpent's Seduction

Lt. Scott Fields stared at his naked torso, and it was hardly a pretty sight. The Nazi officer who had brought him to his chambers had cut off most of his clothing to get them away from his burns. He was left now with only his socks, boxer shorts, and a few scraps of his pants. Beyond this, the Nazi had bound both his hands and legs, but had administered no first aid to his burns.

The pain and the mere two-second glance he could stomach before upchucking over the side of the bed revealed that literally all the skin on the right side of his chest had been seared away. Much of the muscular tissue beneath had been charred so badly that there was no distinguishable pain, only the beginning of what was certain to be a life-ending infection.

His left side was only slightly better off with several gapping slashes where a piece of shrapnel had cut him. His lower torso was fairly intact, but each of his abdominal muscles was bruised in a rainbow of varying shades of black and blue.

As for his face, a field of blisters consumed the right side, and blood still poured from his left eye. Why they had left him here to writhe in agony, half-blind he could not understand. Given the choice, he would have chosen a Nazi plasma bolt to the head in an instant.

"How are you feeling, Lieutenant?"

Fields instantly began searching the shadows of his cabin. He had not heard the door open, or had he seen anyone enter; but in his condition, he hardly trusted his memory. The voice had been cool, feminine, and kind, and a moment later its owner stepped into the light of his bedside lamp.

Even a blind man would have been hard pressed to dismiss her, for she was gorgeous! Her long, ebony hair was loose and flowing across tender shoulders. The curves of her body were revealed neatly beneath her skintight uniform, and her scent – oh, the scent! – was beyond intoxicating. Fields might have been only 16 and half-blind, but oh, wow!

Despite this, he demanded, "What do you want, Captain Bell?"

Bell slipped onto the bed beside him and stroked a hand tenderly across the undamaged side of his face. Had his legs and arms not been bound, he would have moved away from her when she drew closer to him, but he could not. He only hoped his appearance would keep her away, but again it did not. He could only assume she had come here to kill him, but she had no weapons on her person. Rather, she placed a small medical kit on the bed in front of her.

She sounded annoyed as she said, "Somebody should have tended to these wounds a long time ago. If you want something done right, I suppose…Here, let me help you." At that, she opened the kit.

From inside, she retrieved a small white container, and upon opening it, she covered her hands in a green cream that she then began to rub between her two palms. She said,

35

"You'll love this stuff, Lieutenant. Nazi Medical Research and Development has come a long way in the last decade. I'll have you fixed up in no time."

"What's the point?" Fields mumbled.

"Oh, come now, don't be like that. I have no desire to kill you personally."

"Just my captain, right?"

"How well do you really know her?"

"Well enough to trust her and give my life for her without a second thought."

"I see," Bell mused, and she placed both of her hands on the Lieutenant's chest and began to massage the cream into his burns. The sensation was absolutely surreal! Every pleasure center in his body was on fire, and despite his pain and his wounds, he now felt amazing!

"What's in that stuff?"

"I'm not a doctor, but I know it includes artificial endorphins to prompt tissue regeneration while at the same time stimulating the body in every way imaginable. Shall I continue?"

Fields knew the right answer, but he said, "Please do!"

Bell loaded her hands up with more cream, and as she began to work on the Lieutenant's legs, she asked, "So, has your captain told you about me?"

"Not recently, but when I heard your name on the bridge, I remembered reading an old report. You were a rebel once. You had an affair with Captain Morgan of the *Breakaway*. Brooks caught you, and, in revenge, you killed Morgan and betrayed us to the Nazis."

"Funny how the story changes depending on who's doing the telling."

"And how would you tell it?" Scott knew deep within that he couldn't believe a word Bell told him, but right now, with every desire, sensual and otherwise, on overload, he would have gladly kissed the devil on the lips and not regretted it.

"Yes, there was an affair, but it wasn't between Morgan and me. His affair was with Brooks."

"That's not…"

"Before you dismiss it, I would dig a little deeper. I was the one who caught Morgan and your captain being indiscreet. I tried to file a report with Commander Fisher, but Brooks intercepted me before I could. She locked me in a storage closet and filed her own report for transmission back to the Io base. However, in her version, I was the one having the affair with Morgan."

"Either way, Morgan would have been court martialed. Why did he maintain command of the *Breakaway*?"

"You might know from your history that the *Intruder's* last mission as the *Breakaway* was to rescue three rebel officials the Nazis were holding hostage on Earth's subterranean lunar colony."

"I lived there with my parents before it was destroyed by the Nazis."

"Hmm…then you might remember the attack. Well, the mission was of such crucial importance that the *Breakaway* was under a communications blackout. Here, I'm going to start on your face now. How are you doing?"

"I'm on fire…in a great way. I just want to…"

"Oh, I know. Just try to breathe deeply and focus on something else. With such extensive burns, the pleasure sensations you must be feeling right now must be overwhelming, but I am almost done, and they will begin to subside.

"What if I don't want them to?"

"Now, now, Lieutenant, what would your captain think? Anyway, where was I?"

"A communications blackout."

"Right, Brooks' falsified report could not be transmitted until the mission was over, so Morgan remained in command. Sometime later, Brooks returned to retrieve me. She must have gassed me, or drugged me, because the next thing I remember was being in a room of bare rock. Captain Morgan was dead beside me, and I was surrounded by Nazi guards. It was only later that I learned the hostages had been rescued, and I apparently had been abandoned to my fate. In exchange for my life, I gave my rebel secrets to the Nazis. Eventually, I earned their trust and a commission among their ranks."

"That can't be true!"

"Believe what you want. I'm done here regardless."

Fields looked down again, and he saw nothing but healthy skin. All his wounds were gone.

"Is that better?"

"Very much, thank you," he said, gazing into her eyes. There was something hypnotic about them, though he couldn't yet tell if it was the endorphin overload telling him that.

She smiled and walked over to his closet and withdrew a new uniform tunic. She moved back over to him, and kneeling down, she began to untie the ropes that bound his hands. She said, "You'll want to put this on, Lieutenant. You don't want to catch cold."

He took the tunic from her and put it on. She then seized his hands again and bound them. "My apologies, Lieutenant. You understand, I can't allow you to roam free. But I will tell you, I don't plan to kill you. In fact, I had hoped that the two of us would be able to cooperate. I can ensure you; I can be a very grateful woman. Now, why don't you rest? I'll come back in a while." She lingered only a moment longer, enough for him to catch her scent. Then she turned and left the room.

~

In the mess hall, Captain Brooks finished praying with Commander Smith. Leah was awash with tears. Moments earlier, she had accepted Jesus Christ as her Savior. Smith had been one of Brooks' most difficult cases as far as sharing the gift of Salvation was concerned. They had bashed heads more than once, mainly when Brooks had decided to rely on God rather than technology. Now, with Leah as part of her Christian family, this would no longer be an issue. However, her greatest case was yet to be resolved.

Lt. Cmdr. Martinez whispered, "Ever since the service ended, Lt. Brandon hasn't said a word. Not that he ever talked much anyway, but I think we got to him somehow."

Austin looked at Brooks and asked, "So, Captain, what's the next step?"

Brooks drew them all closer to her to keep the Nazis from overhearing and said, "If we're going to retake the ship, I will need everyone I have. That means treating the wounds of all the doctor's patients. I'm going to talk to Brandon."

At his station near the entrance of the mess hall, Lt. Brandon fidgeted with his rifle. The events of the last few hours had all but driven him to the edge. The people aboard this ship had something he wanted, and he had already decided he would take no part in hurting them. He only hoped they could somehow learn to trust him. But, for now, he had to remain a Nazi.

"Lt. Brandon," came a voice.

The man spun around to see Captain Lori Brooks. She had again approached him unnoticed. However, he saw only gentleness, no malice, in her eyes. Uninvited, she sat down on the bench beside him and asked, "How are you, Lieutenant?"

"How am I? Why should you care?"

"Forgive me," she said. "I've been watching you, and I can tell that you don't belong here…with the Nazis I mean."

"What?"

"You are not like any Nazi I have ever met. And I could have sworn that several times during the worship service you seemed almost anxious to take me up on my invitation."

His eyes betrayed him for a liar as he said, "You are mistaken, Captain. Now, leave me alone!"

Brooks held up her hands in surrender and then turned away, knowing that Brandon's Nazi defenses would not last much longer.

~

"Just let it happen, Lieutenant." Those were the last words Fields heard before Captain Jess A. Bell shoved him against the back of his bed and began kissing him!

The kiss was both passionate and sweet, and the artificial endorphins were still so strong within him that refusing her wasn't even a thought in his mind. He felt the warmth and softness of her skin and drew in her potent scent. Here, in the arms of his enemy, he would give away his purity and his heart, and he didn't care. He was hers and, very likely, soon the Nazis' as well.

In a moment, she had unbound his hands, and he felt them move up her back. Now she was unbuttoning his tunic, and…

"I AM THE LORD YOUR GOD!"

"What?"

"WHO LEADS YOU BY THE WAY YOU SHOULD GO!"

"Huh?"

"RESIST THE DEVIL AND HE WILL FLEE FROM YOU!"

"Lord?"

"What is it?" Bell asked.

"This is wrong! I shouldn't be doing this."

"Oh, come on, live a little, Scott. May I call you *Scott*?"

"Actually, I would prefer that you call me *Lieutenant*. Now get off of me!"

She touched his lips with a slender finger and whispered, "No one will ever know. Just relax." Then she pressed him back on the bed and kissed him again, but something had changed. Moments earlier, her lips had tasted like honey. Now, for some reason, they tasted like rotting fish. And her scent, once as fragrant as perfume, now smelled like baked cow dung. In that instant, it seemed every last endorphin – artificial and otherwise – in his body died.

"Stop! Stop now!"

"Why?"

"For one thing, you threatened to kill my captain and my crew. And you told me a story only an idiot would believe. But more specifically, you are about to take something from me that Christ says we should save for only one person."

"Christ?" Bell chuckled. "Are the rebels still holding on to that fairytale?"

Scott did not answer, and Bell continued, "It's a natural biological process, Lieutenant. I don't understand why there should be a rule against it, or the harm in sharing it with more than one person."

"I don't expect you could understand, but I also don't expect *that* is what you really want from me."

She took hold of one of his now free arms and said, "You're right, Lieutenant. What I want is for you to show me how to override the helm lockout. The helm is your station after all. I'm sure you would know how to do it. And if you help me, I can promise you'll have a powerful place among the Nazis. Just imagine what your life will be like. Forget about Brooks. She nearly got you killed, and as for your God, He's just holding you back. As a Nazi, you could indulge in any kind of pleasure you might desire, and you will have power beyond your imagination."

A devilish smirk formed on Scott's face, and he drew close to her ear and whispered seductively, "Oh, really? Tell me more."

Bell smiled and drew her body back toward him. He wrapped his arms around her and kissed her. It was a full and passionate kiss. One that sent vibrations to every corner of their bodies. *The serpent had seduced her prey.*

But then…

Lt. Fields let his lips linger on hers a moment longer. Then, with all the force he could muster, he plunged his teeth into Bell's lower lip. Even though the blood pouring into his mouth had a bitter taste, the sensation was a sweet one. He did not stop biting until his teeth had ripped all the way through her lip. And when she finally managed to wrench herself away, her blood had covered his face.

For a moment, Jess A. Bell's eyes flared in the dark, and Fields knew it would not be beneath her dignity to kill him then and there. But it would be worth it just to see the look on her face right now. It was one of defeat, rage, and betrayal doing a macabre waltz along her cheek bones. Fields was not surprised when the blow from her fist came. What surprised him was how far it sent him flying. He flew straight from the bed and slammed onto the floor.

"Have it your way! You can die with the rest of them!"

~

Lt. Brandon sat tormented by the words of Captain Brooks. Every part of him was telling him he should accept her offer, but his fear was holding him back. However, the more he thought about it, the more sense deserting to the rebel side of the war made. After all, even if there was a chance of him getting killed, with a captain like Bell it would not be long before he was killed anyway. At least with the rebels, he would be giving his life for something that mattered, and if Brooks was right about Christ, he would be giving his soul over to Someone eternal. Ultimately, there was only one choice to make.

~

"How do you think Lt. Fields is doing?" asked Klaus Martinez.

"I don't know. I haven't heard..." Brooks started, but then she stopped as someone new approached the huddle of her senior officers. It was Daniel Brandon.

"Captain, I changed my mind. I will help you."

Brooks' smile threatened to leap off her face. She said, "Welcome to the family, Lieutenant. Now, come closer. We've been working on a plan. Here is exactly what we need you to do…"

Chapter 5
Providence

L t. Brandon was unsure about his new captain's plan, but he was not about to question it. He said, "Now let me get this straight. I find a way to distract the rest of the guards, so that Dr. Radcliff can sneak his patients to the sickbay and treat them properly."

Brooks replied, "That's right. After that, you and I will sneak to the armory and bring tachyon rifles for the rest of the crew. You told me Captain Bell only brought over forty officers. The *Intruder* has over a hundred currently onboard. Once we're properly armed, we will be more than a match for them."

Brandon was skeptical, but Commander Eli, who was now mostly recovered, was the one to voice concern. "Captain, we underestimated the Nazis once, and they took over our ship."

"If the result was Commander Smith's salvation, along with about a dozen others, as well as Daniel finding a new home with us, it was well worth it."

Turning to Brandon, Brooks said, "Lieutenant, get those guards out of here. We should get this going."

Brandon nodded and moved away from his new friends. For some reason, the other guards had remained oblivious to his less than covert meeting with the rebels. He couldn't explain it, but it had to be one of those miracles Captain Brooks had been talking about.

He approached a small group of guards and said, "Ensigns, I want the five of you to go up to the next deck and access the holoviewer technology control center. Remove the primary processors and projection systems and bring them back here."

One of them, a dark headed ensign named Sawyer, asked, "Why?"

"Just before we boarded the *Intruder*, Captain Bell ordered me to repair the holoviewer on the *Feline's Claw's*. You know how impatient the captain is. I can probably jury-rig our system back into something usable, but not before she loses patience with me. A new system would save me a lot of grief, but I'll need some time to see if it's compatible."

"Why do you need it now?"

"What else have I got to do?"

"Only guard over a hundred prisoners, sir."

"Ah, well, rank has its privileges. The captain wouldn't appreciate me leaving my post, but you can go get the system for me."

Sawyer was still not convinced. He said, "The rest of the guards are now on sleep rotation. We're the only ones left. Do you honestly expect us to believe you can guard over a hundred rebels all by yourself?"

Brandon hugged his rifle flatly across his chest and said, "That's right; I do. You are looking at the officer who was at the top of his class in Nazi defensive tactics. Not to mention the fact that I earned my present rank by taking out an entire squad of rebels. If any of Brooks' crew try to get past me, I'll blow their brains across the carpet."

The ensign protested, "But Captain Bell said not to kill any of them!"

Brandon rolled his eyes in annoyance and then said, "If I hear one more complaint, it's going to be your brains greasing this carpet! Now get going! It will take all five of you to carry the system down here."

"Very well, *sir*. But if we can't excise it within ten minutes, we're coming back. The captain still outranks you, *sir*, and I want to stay on her good side."

"Does she have one of those?" Brandon quipped. "Very well; understood. Now get going!"

Sawyer nodded and directed his men out of the room. Brandon watched until they were well down the corridor; then he turned and signaled to Brooks. Then Brooks signaled to Radcliff, and, with the help of several other crew members, the doctor began to carry the wounded from the room.

Brooks and Brandon stood guard until all of Radcliff's patients were gone. Then the captain took hold of Brandon's rifle.

"What are you doing?"

"Back down those Nazi instincts, Danny. Right now, this will be more useful elsewhere."

Reluctantly, Brandon surrendered his gun. Brooks tossed it to Eli and said, "Just in case you run into any trouble, Commander." Then she gestured to Brandon and said, "Now, let's get moving! The clock is ticking."

Outside, the corridor was an ungodly black, penetrated only by a few flashing, red beacons. Brandon asked, "Which way?"

"The armory is two decks below. This way!" Brooks replied, and they headed off at a run.

~

"Ah…ah, come on!" Fields cursed as he struggled with the locking mechanism confining him to his cabin. He had spent the better part of the last five years studying the Nazi technology aboard the Space Port, and he liked to think he had become fairly proficient in decoding even the most complicated technologies, but this locking system, for whatever reason, was eluding him. Whether it was the residual effects of the endorphins blurring his concentration, the possibility that the Nazis had really stepped up their technology, or the very real threat of Bell returning at any moment to kill him, he simply could not clear his mind enough to crack this code.

"Stop where you are!" sounded a husky voice from out in the corridor. Fields guessed it was the guard outside his door.

"Put your weapon on the ground now!"

He recognized that voice instantly. "Captain!"

"Like hell!"

"Have it your way!"

THUD!

"What the…" Fields stuttered and watched as his cabin door slid open and the limp form of a Nazi ensign slumped across the threshold.

"Lieutenant, we could use your help!"

"Captain! How did you get free?"

"It's a long story for another time. For the moment, we have to get moving. I would like you to me…"

"Captain, look out!"

"Lieutenant, no!" Brooks shouted, but she was too late to stop two well-aimed fists from sending Daniel Brandon to the floor.

Brandon gasped hard to catch his breath, and then he demanded, "What is wrong with him?"

Brooks sighed and said, "Lt. Daniel Brandon, I'd like you to meet Lt. Scott Fields, my helmsman."

"Charmed, I'm sure," sneered Brandon, rising from the floor.

Fields looked to his captain in confusion, "What is going on?"

"That is also a long story, but we're on a clock. Lt. Brandon is with us now. Is that understood, Mr. Fields?"

"Yes, Captain."

"Good! Now, I want you to go to the armory with Lt. Brandon. Take enough weapons back to the mess hall to arm the crew."

"The whole crew?"

"Yes, there should be more than enough weapons there."

"How will we carry them?"

"Last time I checked, there were four antigravity carts in the armory. That should do the trick, but you'll have to be careful and quick."

"Right. And where are you going?" he asked.

"To the engine room to run some tests on the computer. When we retake the ship, we'll need to know to whom the helm lockout code belongs. I'll use the auxiliary computer in the engine room to find out. Now, get to work," Brooks ordered and then sprinted into the darkness.

A moment later, both Fields and Brandon were on their way as well. Brandon said, "That's quite a jab you've got there, Lieutenant."

Scott smiled and replied, "Five years training with Commander Eli will do it every time. He was a professional MMA fighter before the war. When he became our first officer five years ago, he insisted on training me and several of the other younger officers."

Brandon commented, "Well, from that right hook you gave me, I'd say the rebels are lucky to have you both."

Fields smiled and said, "Well, by the time today is over, I imagine they will be saying the same thing about you."

~

Commander Eli clasped his hands harder around the Nazi rifle and gazed out the viewport. Smith stood beside him, and he asked, "Do you think we can do this?"

Smith put a hand on his shoulder and simply said, "Yes." And for whatever reason might have possessed her, she kissed Eli on the cheek. Then she turned from him and headed for Loso as the commander looked on in utter shock. He had pursued her from the moment they had met over six years ago. Both were in their 30s by that point, with few prospects for a spouse – not that that was a huge concern during this unending war – but she never seemed to want to give him the time of day, and their conversations were always strictly professional. Now, for whatever reason, she was starting to warm up to him, and he was not about to complain.

When Smith reached Loso, she asked, "Any luck?"

Loso shook his cybernetic head. When the Nazis had first taken control of the *Intruder*, they had forcefully removed his cybernetic laser. Now, with spare components from about the mess hall, he was attempting to fashion another.

Smith was disappointed, but not for long. Only moments later, Lieutenants Brandon and Fields burst into the room with two antigravity carts filled with weapons.

"I was getting worried about you, Lieutenant Brandon. Your Nazi counterparts were supposed to be back seven minutes ago."

"Yeah, we ran into them in the corridor," Lt. Fields reported. "They won't be an issue anymore."

Smith nodded in understanding and then took charge. "All right, everyone, listen up. By now, the captain will be close to accessing the helm decryption code, but that will do little good if she doesn't have a ship to navigate. I think it is time we remedied that situation."

She turned to Fields and said, "Scott, go and tell the captain to meet us on the bridge in ten minutes. Lieutenant Brandon, go to the bridge, but don't do anything. I'll still need you to be a Nazi for a little while longer." She nodded at them, and both men headed off. Then she turned to the remaining crew and said, "The rest of you are with me. Gear up!"

~

The battle to reach the bridge was not a long one. Eli counted the bodies as they went along. By the time they reached the corridor outside the bridge, at least two dozen Nazis were dead or dying. Just before reaching their objective, Smith halted her troops and said, "We've got to wait for the captain." Then she directed them all into hiding places.

~

On the bridge, Commander Pfeiffer sounded, "Captain Bell, I'm detecting rebel soldiers moving through the ship!

They have retaken several decks and are converging on the bridge!"

Bell, in Brooks' chair, muttered an extremely profane curse - made all the more acerbic by her lacerated lower lip. Then she ordered, "Lieutenant Brandon, seal off the bridge."

Brandon acknowledged her order, but he did not carry it out. Unaware of this, Bell moved down to her helmsman and asked, "Any luck in overriding the lockout?"

The officer at the rebuilt helm had been about to say no, but when a beacon began to flash, he grinned and exclaimed, "Yes, Captain! The sub-LS thrusters just came back online."

She touched him gingerly and said, "Take us out of here." Then she returned to the command chair, crossed her legs and smirked at Captain Brooks' failure.

~

"Commander Smith, are you ready?"

Leah turned to see her captain. "Yes, Captain. Did you figure out the code?"

"Ironically, it ended up being mine. I reinitiated the helm. I imagine the Nazis know by now, but it doesn't matter." She turned to her crew and said, "You have all done well. Go to your stations and secure them. This will all be over soon."

As the junior officers headed off, Brooks turned to her bridge crew and ordered, "We're going to take back what belongs to us. Have your weapons ready; we're going in!"

~

"Brandon! You were supposed to seal the bridge! I'll kill you for this!" Jess A. Bell spat.

"That's not likely," Brooks broke in. "It's over, Captain. Surrender my ship, and you will not be harmed."

"Brandon, kill her! I may yet spare you."

Brandon made no move, and she shouted, "Brandon, now!"

Only seconds later, she suddenly realized why he had not moved. His weapon was trained on her.

"I'm sorry, Captain. I don't take orders from you anymore."

Bell's eyes boiled into him. She was angrier than he had ever seen her before, and he knew people who angered her never lived to regret it. She screamed to the rest of her men, "Take them down!"

The rest of the Nazis were quick to respond to their captain's order, but it was useless. Squeezing the triggers of their guns, they let out a series of muffled curses, and Brandon knew why. "You'll find those useless. I drained the power cells."

Brooks commanded, "Get them out of here."

And with that Eli and Smith began to do so. Bell remained the only Nazi on the bridge, and Brooks explained, "Lt. Brandon has come to realize that no force can hope to overcome a God-fearing people. Daniel is with us now, and you are going spend the rest of your life in a rebel prison camp. Too bad you couldn't come to the same realization he did."

Bell didn't speak, but she kept her fiery eyes fixed on Brandon - a look that told him she would give anything to see him dead. But he wanted to prove to her once and for all that he was no longer under her control.

Brooks instructed, "Loso, take her out of here!"

However, Brandon protested, "Captain, let me do that."

Brooks let a frown cascade across her face, but she wanted to show her trust in Brandon. She nodded and said, "Go." Then she directed the rest of her officers back to their stations.

~

"You know, it's a shame you decided to turn traitor. I had you in mind for a promotion when this was over. You were turning out to be a valuable officer. God only knows how good you would be to me in other areas?" Bell said. Though she was currently in the sites of Brandon's rifle, she still acted as if she were in complete control.

"Don't speak to me about God! You know nothing of Him."

She shrugged and admitted, "Perhaps, but I know enough to tell you that Hell is where we all end up in the end. It's only a matter of how we get there."

Brandon did not even process this remark. Not that he would have had the time, because the entire deck suddenly bucked beneath him and threw him into the bulkhead! He crashed to the floor and fumbled for his weapon in vain as it flew away down the corridor.

In an instant, Bell had seized it. She trained it on him and unleashed a fiery energy bolt. It missed him by mere inches as he whirled away. The deck bucked again, slamming him into the wall. As he recovered, his eyes fell upon a single control box. In bold red bold letters, the control read, *Airlock 43*.

"Thank you, Lord!" Brandon silently prayed, even as he heard the power cell of Bell's weapon again reach its full

charge. He turned back to his former captain, his face now drenched in sweat and his breathing labored.

Her countenance, on the other hand, was cold and stiff, punctuated only by a fire in her dragon-like eyes that Brandon was certain far too many had seen the very instant they died. Tossing a loose strand of hair back over her shoulder, she said, "Goodbye, Lieutenant!"

But she was too late. Brandon slammed his fist into the airlock control. As her rifle blast exploded against the bulkhead next to him, a hatch at the far end of the corridor rushed open with a serpentine hiss. Brandon watched as a river of toxic gases invaded the corridor, even as he wrapped his arms around a nearby pipe. He was not about to let himself be sucked into Jupiter's hellish atmosphere. Bell was not so fortunate.

One moment, she stood poised with the rifle a few meters from him. The next, she was clutching her hands around the edges of the airlock as the demonic storms of Jupiter's atmosphere pulled upon her. She bellowed a scream that would have put all the banshees of Hell to shame as the searing gases of Jupiter's atmosphere began to boil her flesh. She wailed all the more as pieces of her face began to peel away. Soon Brandon could see the bones of her skull, and he turned away as blood began to pour from her eyes. When Bell could see the last of her ravaged hands were nearly dissolved, she screamed one last curse, "I'll see you in Hell, Brandon!" Then she released her grip and allowed the planet to consume her.

Resealing the airlock, Brandon quipped, "Actually, I think I'll be heading in the opposite direction!"

~

Lt. Fields complained, "It's no use, Captain! I can't take us any higher. The engines have completely corroded in the atmosphere."

Brooks asked, "How far are we from orbit?"

Eli, back at his post, reported, "Only twenty kilometers, Captain."

"Options?" the captain asked.

Smith, at tactical, replied, "I can't think of…" Then she paused and stared at her panel. A tiny green blip was moving slowly across the screen.

She exclaimed, "Captain, I'm reading a large asteroid in low orbit! It's probably a remnant from an old moon breakup. If we can latch our grappling tower onto it, its current velocity should be able to pull us out of here."

Brooks had never heard of anything quite like what Smith was suggesting, so she asked Loso, "Can we do it?"

Loso responded, "The asteroid is twenty-seven kilometers from us, and the towing cable is only thirty kilometers long. There would be virtually no margin for error."

Brooks met the eyes of her bridge crew before she commanded, "Do it!"

Loso complied, and they all turned their attention back to their tiny scanner displays. They watched as the grappling cable soared upward toward the asteroid. Seconds passed and then more seconds. Finally, the cable was within range, and in that last second, their fates were sealed.

Smith struggled to hold back a stream of profanities before she said, "Captain, the tower missed. The asteroid is moving out of range."

Brooks' face went slack. They were all going to die, consumed by the fiery hell that was Jupiter's atmosphere.

But then…

"Captain, I'm detecting a rebel TSJ! It just took hold of our towing cable and is pulling us out of the atmosphere!" Fields shouted, in almost giddy amazement.

Brooks could hardly believe it herself. She dared not speak for fear, but soon enough Fields' report was confirmed as the ship jolted, and they could hear the steady retraction of the grappler as the *Intruder* ascended from its fiery grave.

Brooks ordered, "Contact that jet. I'd like to thank her pilot."

Eli tried to comply, but confused, he reported, "Captain, the TSJ is gone! There is no sign of it." Then he studied his board further and continued, "I am detecting two rebel ships, though. They are the *Snapper* and the *Destiny*. We are receiving a hail. It's from Admiral Carter."

Standing, Brooks instructed, "Put him on the holoviewer."

After a moment, the age-worn image of Admiral Carter took shape on the screen. He said, *"Welcome back, Captain. We were beginning to get worried. Shortly after you entered the atmosphere, backup arrived, and we destroyed the Feline's Claw. But we could not enter the atmosphere to find you. Our vessels are not as advanced as the Intruder."*

Brooks smiled, "I think we can remedy that situation, Admiral. Oh, and by the way, thank you for towing us out of the atmosphere with your TSJ."

Carter looked puzzled and said, *"Captain, none of our jets towed you out, nor would a TSJ be capable."*

Brooks was equally confused. She started, "Then how did we..." Then she smiled in realization and silently prayed, *"Thank you, Lord!"*

Carter continued, *"Captain, if you will dock your ship on Io, we can begin her repairs, and I..."*

Brooks interrupted him, "Admiral, if you would not mind, I'd like you to come aboard the *Intruder*. There is someone here I'd like you to meet."

~

Lt. Brandon found his new rebel uniform to be rather itchy. Just before he stepped onto the bridge, he indulged in one last intense scratch. When he came onto the deck, he noticed a number of officers he had met already, and a new, older man with the word *ADMIRAL* in brass letters on his collar. Next to him stood Captain Brooks.

Brooks looked concerned, and she said, "Lt. Brandon, I'm afraid I have bad news. I'm going to have to demote you."

"Captain?"

Brandon wondered what he could have done wrong to earn a demotion, but Brooks' face instantly warmed into a smile, and she said, "Consider it a fresh start on your new life with us."

Then she stood up straight and addressed him formally, "Lt. Daniel Brandon of the New International Nazi Confederation, for services rendered to the Rebellion during a time of crisis, I am honored to grant you the rank of *ensign* in the Anti-Nazi Rebellion Forces, with all the rights and privileges thereto."

Though in all respects his new rank was inferior to his old one, Brandon still felt ten feet taller. And this feeling increased when the senior crew began to argue.

Fields said, "I intend to recruit Ensign Brandon onto my helmsmen's staff. I am sure he has a Nazi maneuver or two up his sleeve that would come in handy."

Smith disagreed, "He would be of more use at tactical. His knowledge of Nazi weaponry could be crucial."

Then Loso jumped in, "I believe I could make better use of him in the Intelligence Department. His overall knowledge of the Nazis would go a long way in enhancing our chances of victory."

Brandon threw up his arms and said, "Easy everyone, I think I can make time for all of you. Just let me have a day off first, okay?" They all smiled at that, and Brandon smiled too. For the first time, in a long time, he was truly part of a family.

After

"So, how are the rebels doing?" Spikey Moonbeam asked.

The 11-year-old Scotty Fields stared at him blankly. The *Prism's Echo* was now closed and in the inventor's hand. "What?" Scotty asked dryly.

"That's where you were right?"

Scotty only shook his head, still only vaguely aware of his surroundings.

"Scotty! Snap out of it!" Sparkey demanded.

That shook the boy loose from his reverie, and he said, "Wow! Sorry, guys. I really got lost this time. I wasn't even myself – I was Lt. Fields, and boy, has he gotten buff."

"I take it the war goes well?" Spikey said.

"I guess…in a way. The rebels are on the up, but that was a very intense *mission*. Actually…somewhere in there…I got my first kiss, though I don't think it's one I will want to remember."

Gloria perked up, and she said, "Really? Do tell!"

Scotty squirmed, "Maybe another time. But I also met two traitors. One betrayed the rebels for the Nazis, and the other betrayed the Nazis for the rebels. The former is now dead, but I think the latter has a very bright future ahead of him."

"That's good," Spikey said with half a smile.

"Yes, but I also think that Lt. Fields and Captain Brooks have quite a lot to talk about."

"What do you mean?" Gloria asked.

"It's just…oh, never mind. How are you doing, Spikey? Gloria told me what day this is."

Spikey nodded and said, "It's hard to believe it's been 17 years. A lot of good friends died that night, and we will always miss them."

Gloria drew near to her husband, and he wrapped his arm around her waist. Scotty and Sparkey also joined them, and soon they were all locked in an intense embrace. Finally, Spikey asked, "Do you know what I think the best part about days like this are?"

"What's that, Dad?" Sparkey asked.

"No matter what bad things may happen in this life, at the end of the day, I am just extremely grateful to still be part of a family!"

About the Author

David Scott Fields II is an author, teacher, publisher, and Christian journalist currently residing in Jupiter, Florida. At the time of this publication, his works include the novels *Staranana, Lizard Face, Old Covenant, New Covenant, The Noble Dragons,* and *The Emperor's Passage* in the *Chronicles of the Imagination* series. Additionally, he has published the novellas *The Betrayal of Kelcott,* also from the *Chronicles of the Imagination* series, and *The Prism's Echo, Salvage,* and *Allegiance* from the *Parallel Encounters* series. His educational writing includes the children's writing workbook *Green Elephant* and curriculum supplements for several classic pieces of literature.

In addition to his writing career, Mr. Fields has served for decades as a teacher in schools in Oregon, Alaska, and Florida. As a Christian teacher and writer, Mr. Fields seeks to remind the young people in his life that God is alive. His goal, above all else, is that his life will be a testament for Jesus Christ and that his writings will help bring many people into a saving relationship with their Creator.

The Adventure Continues in Book 4...
Parallel Encounters:
Retrospect

Chronicles of the Imagination
By David Scott Fields II

Faith, friendship, and family all collide in this action-packed and Christ-honoring fantasy adventure!

Scan to Learn More

Check out these *Classroom Classics* from *Thrive Christian Press*:

Rudyard Kipling's The Jungle Book – Enhanced Classroom Edition
ISBN – 978-0615705859

From Mowgli's relentless battle against the man-eating tiger Shere Khan to Rikki-Tikki-Tavi's great war against the sinister cobras Nag and Nagaina, Rudyard Kipling's classic *The Jungle Book* has been filling our lives with excitement for more than a century now. No personal library is complete without this timeless novel, and this edition enhanced for use in the classroom is a must have for any teacher about to embark on this literary adventure.

Steven Crane's The Red Badge of Courage - Enhanced Classroom Edition
ISBN – 978-0615808123

How does a coward become a hero? Henry Fleming is about to face that very question. Though he had, "...dreamed of battles all his life...", he soon finds that a soldier's life is more than he bargained for, and a single wrong decision runs the risk of branding him a coward for what little of his life he thinks he has left. Will he ultimately find the hero within, earning, if necessary, his own red badge of courage, or will he die a coward?

Sir Arthur Conan Doyle's The Hound of the Baskervilles –
Enhanced Classroom Edition
ISBN – 9780615831701

There is a realm in which the most experienced of detectives is helpless – The Supernatural, and master detective Sherlock Holmes is about to plunge headfirst into that realm in this stunning adventure. *The Hound of the Baskervilles* takes Holmes and Dr. Watson to the Baskerville Estate where a mysterious hound of Hell has caused the deaths of many members of the Baskerville family. Will Holmes be able to crack this case before the latest heir to the Baskerville fortune meets his demise?

Mark Twain's The Adventures of Tom Sawyer – Enhanced Classroom Edition
ISBN – 978-0692021477

In this latest edition of Mark Twain's classic, *The Adventures of Tom Sawyer*, we are once again reunited with one of the most beloved literary characters of all time. Tom Sawyer is sure to bring out the rascal in any of us and leave us with a thirst for adventure with the turn of every page. This enhanced edition includes journal prompts, study and discussion questions, and vocabulary activities great for use in the classroom.

Mark Twain's The Prince and the Pauper – Enhanced Classroom Edition
ISBN – 978-0692389096

Edward Tudor, the Prince of Wales, was born destined to be the king of all England. Tom Canty was born in squalor and destined for a life of misery in the slums of the London streets. However, a chance encounter between these two doppelgängers will send destiny into a tailspin as Edward and Tom suddenly and unexpectedly trade places. This enhanced edition includes journal prompts, study and discussion questions, and vocabulary activities great for use in the classroom.

Jack London's White Fang - Enhanced Classroom Edition
ISBN – 978-0692678480

"It was the Wild, the savage, frozen-hearted Northland Wild." The wolf White Fang was born of that wilderness, but at the hands of man he will learn to become the most ruthless of killers, until the kindness of one man changes things forever. This new edition of Jack London's classic *White Fang* comes enhanced with great extras for the classroom.

Also available from *Thrive Christian Press:*

Chronicles of the Imagination: The Betrayal of Kelcott
ISBN - 978-1945995118

Revenge! Cold, Sweet Revenge! Every race has its traitors, and the people of Staranana are no exception. Set 15 years before the events of *Chronicles of the Imagination: Staranana,* readers will find themselves transported back to one of the most heartbreaking chapters in the planet's deep and bloody history. A time when a trusted friend became a bitter enemy. Families will be destroyed, the truth will be abandoned, and death will run rampant, but in the end, God's truth endures, and hope survives.

Parallel Encounters: The Prism's Echo
ISBN - 978-0692329962

Parallel Encounters: The Prism's Echo takes us to Staranana less than a week after Scotty and his friends have returned from the biblical past. With rest being the word of the day, the Staranananians soon find themselves in the vast halls of the Palace's library where a mysterious book called *The Prism's Echo* is brought to their attention. To the naked eye, it is just a book, but to a reader with the right question, it opens the door to infinite possible realities. Unfortunately for Scotty, the wrong question lands him stranded in an alternate universe where humanity has fallen to a space age Nazi regime.

Parallel Encounters: Salvage
ISBN - 978-0692352359

Four tense but quiet years have passed for the rebels since they captured the Nazi Space Port. As the station's supplies and energy draw near to total depletion, hope comes in the form of a mysterious and evidently abandoned alien spacecraft floating dead in space. Called the *Rimcha*, Brooks hopes to salvage the alien vessel and incorporate its resources into those of the rebellion. But there's a problem; the Nazis have spotted the alien ship too, and now the race is on to see who will capture the vessel first. If it's the rebellion, Earth may finally be liberated, but if it's the Nazis, any hope of further resistance may be crushed forever.